SIX DEGREES OF SPORTS

SIX DEGREES°
OF PEYTON MANNING
CONNECTING FOOTBALL STARS

BY HANS HETRICK

CAPSTONE PRESS
a capstone imprint

Sports Illustrated Kids Six Degrees of Sports are published by Capstone Press,
1710 Roe Crest Drive, North Mankato, Minnesota 56003. www.capstonepub.com

Library of Congress Cataloging-in-Publication Data
Cataloging information on file with the Library of Congress
ISBN 978-1-4914-2145-1

Editorial Credits

Nate LeBoutillier, editor; Ted Williams, designer; Eric Gohl, media researcher;
Katy LaVigne, production specialist

Photo Credits

CrialImages.com: Jay Robert Nash Collection, 17; Dreamstime: Jerry Coli, 12 (Smith), 16 (top), 18
(Namath), 32 (bottom); Library of Congress: 24 (Thorpe); Newscom: Ai Wire Photo Service, 23,
Everett Collection, 36 (Hutson), 41, Icon SMI/John McDonough, 30 (Lott), Icon SMI/Sporting
News Archives, 35, Icon SMI/TSN, 30 (Jones), Icon Sports Media, cover (Starr), 11 (bottom),
SportsChrome, 12 (Brown), SportsChrome/Tony Tomsic, 6 (Starr); Sports Illustrated: Al Tielemans,
12 (background), 18 (Luck), 20 (bottom), 21, 24 (McNabb, background), 26 (top), 28, 37, Andy Hayt,
cover (Montana, Rice), 6 (Montana), 9 (bottom), 12 (Payton), 24 (Jackson), 29 (top), 30 (White), 34
(top), Bob Rosato, 27, Damian Strohmeyer, 40 (top), David E. Klutho, 18 (background), 20 (top),
24 (Gonzalez), 30 (Watt), 33, 36 (Johnson, Moss), 38, Heinz Kluetmeier, 6 (Rice), 10, 16 (bottom),
24 (Sanders), 30 (Taylor), 34 (bottom), John Biever, 18 (Favre), John Iacono, 12 (Sanders), 15, 18
(Marino), 22 (top), John W. McDonough, 1, 7, 12 (Lynch), 31, 36 (Fitzgerald, background), 39
(bottom), Peter Read Miller, 12 (Tomlinson), 14 (bottom), 36 (Thomas), 39 (top), Robert Beck, cover
(P. Manning), 4–5, 6 (P. Manning, background), 8 (top), 13, 18 (Brady), 30 (Sherman, background),
32 (top, background), Simon Bruty, cover (E. Manning), 6 (E. Manning), 9 (top), 14 (top), 19, 20
(background), 22 (background), 24 (Griffin), 25, 26 (bottom), 28 (background), Walter Iooss Jr.,
cover (Bradshaw), 6 (Bradshaw), 11 (top), 18 (Tarkenton), 22 (bottom), 36 (Swann), 40 (bottom);
Wikimedia: Public Domain, 29 (bottom)

Design Elements

Shutterstock

Sources Quotes:

Page 8: Dave Anderson. "There's No Shuffle in His Step." 1 Feb. 2007. http://www.nytimes.
com/2007/02/01/sports/football/01anderson.html?_r=0. Page 11: "History of the Ice Bowl."
ProFootballHallofFame.com. http://www.profootballhof.com/history/decades/1960s/ice_bowl.
aspx. Page 16: "Walter Payton: A Football Life." From NFL Network's series "A Football Life."
Aired 13 Oct. 2011. http://www.nfl.com/videos/a-football-life/09000d5d8231a856/A-Football-
Life-The-heart-of-Walter. Page 21: "Brett Favre: Thanks for the Memories." NFL Videos. http://
www.nfl.com/videos?videoId=09000d5d802f9978. Page 29: "Jim Thorpe begins Olympic Triathlon."
History.com. http://www.history.com/this-day-in-history/jim-thorpe-begins-olympic-triathlon.
Page 32: "What Makes Richard Sherman Tick?" RealClearSports.com. http://www.realclearsports.
com/2014/01/21/what_makes_richard_sherman_tick_117542.html. Page 33: Tania Ganguli. "The
Life and Times of J.J. Watt." *The Houston Chronicle*. 13 October 2012. http://www.chron.com/
sports/texans/article/The-life-and-times-of-J-J-Watt-3945755.php. Page 34 (top): "Reggie White
Ranked No. 7 All-time." Philly.com. http://www.philly.com/philly/blogs/dneagles/Reggie_
White_ranked_No_7_all_time_.html. Page 34 (bottom): "Lawrence Taylor, the Giants' Crazed
Dog." CBSsports.com. http://www.cbssports.com/nfl/eye-on-football/23280033/watch-lawrence-
taylor-the-giants-crazed-dog. Page 39: "Fitzgerald Continues Meteoric Rise." Larry-Fitzgerald.com.
http://larry-fitzgerald.com/jr/index.php?option=com_content&task=view&id=98&Itemid=1

Printed in the United States of America in Stevens Point, Wisconsin.
112014   008479WZS15

TABLE OF CONTENTS

REMINDS ME OF . . .

Peyton Manning drops back to pass. Holding the ball like a prize, he scans the gridiron, taking in the defense's reactions to his receivers' darts and cuts. Pass rushers, trying to bring him down, bull their way toward Manning. Then Manning makes his decision and with a flash of his arm launches a pass downfield. The ball spirals like a dream and lands in his wideout's hands, another six points for Manning's team. The fact that you're in disbelief shows that Manning has done more than just help his team to another touchdown. He has brought you to your feet—or to your knees—and coaxed a roar from your throat—unless it left you speechless. And whether you say it out loud or not, what you're thinking is, ***I've never seen that before***.

But someone has seen it before. This is just about the time your father says,

"Reminds me of Joe Montana."

To which your grandfather, once upon a time, might have said to him,

"Reminds me of Bart Starr."

Maybe it was an uncle or an aunt who made the comparison. It could have been anyone, right? One element of sports that trickles down through the ages is that we love to connect the players of the game. We measure greatness in sports by the records we keep. But we also measure greatness by way of comparison and contrast. We bring together what may be separate by remembering, *Hey, those guys played together for a couple seasons on the same team*, or, *Hey, that guy actually broke the other guy's record!* These types of connections are what this book is all about.

So whether you connect one great player to the next in barbershops or coffee shops, this book is for you. Whether you strike up debate in back rooms, parlor rooms, living rooms, chat rooms, or lunchrooms, on the streets or in the bleachers, with your friends or foes or teachers, this Six Degrees of Sports book is for you. Enjoy it, and make your own connections.

CHAPTER ONE

TERRY BRADSHAW
Born and raised in Louisiana like the Manning brothers.

ELI MANNING
Son of NFL great Archie Manning, along with older brother Peyton.

JOE MONTANA
Led teams to four Super Bowl victories, as did Bradshaw.

SIX DEGREES
OF PEYTON MANNING

JERRY RICE
Blazing speedster caught 55 TD passes from Montana in 49ers heyday.

BART STARR
Super Bowl MVP like Jerry Rice.

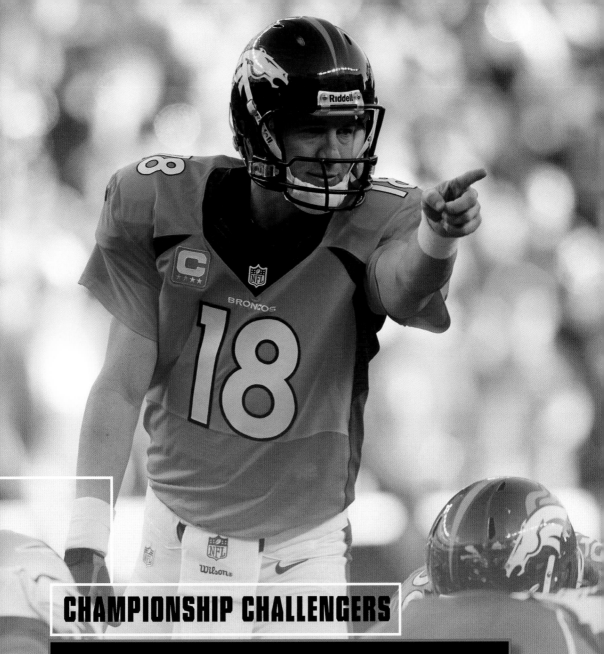

CHAMPIONSHIP CHALLENGERS

National Football League (NFL) greats are created during the Super Bowl. When the championship is on the line, NFL greats make the play. They break a tackle for extra yards. They throw a pinpoint pass between two defenders. They force a turnover. NFL greats are at their best when they are up against the best.

BRONCOS

PEYTON MANNING
▶ Quarterback

HEIGHT: 6-5   **WEIGHT:** 230 lbs.
BORN: 3/24/1976, New Orleans, La.
SCOUTING REPORT: Slices up defenses with precise passing and pregame preparation.

Before ▶ **Peyton Manning** takes a snap, he looks like a crazy, overgrown bird. He flaps his arms, wiggles his fingers, and shouts. Peyton preparing for flight. What's he doing? He's putting his teammates in position to win. Peyton Manning is a master of analyzing any defense in order to take advantage of its weaknesses.

He also has a great arm and incredible instincts. He can hang in the pocket and slip through the most furious pass rush. And he throws a perfect pass nearly every time.

In 2007 Peyton led the Indianapolis Colts to victory in Super Bowl XLI. He picked apart an excellent Chicago Bears defense, earning the Super Bowl MVP in the Colts' 29–17 win. "You're not going to fool Peyton Manning," explained Brian Urlacher, Chicago Bears Pro Bowl linebacker.

Manning and the Colts lost the 2009 season's Super Bowl to the New Orleans Saints, yet Manning played well, throwing for 333 yards. Manning made the Super Bowl a third time with a new team, the Denver Broncos, following the 2013 season. The Broncos lost to the Seattle Seahawks, but Manning set a Super Bowl record with 34 complete passes.

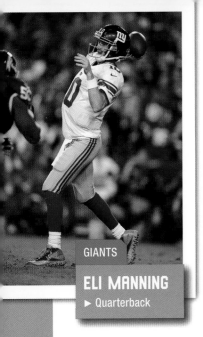

HEIGHT: 6-4   WEIGHT: 218 lbs.
BORN: 1/3/1981, New Orleans, La.
SCOUTING REPORT: Has great bloodlines and stays cool in the pocket in the biggest of games.

GIANTS

ELI MANNING
▶ Quarterback

▶ **Eli Manning** always keeps his cool, even in the Super Bowl. In 2008 Eli's New York Giants were trailing the undefeated New England Patriots 14–10 late in Super Bowl XLII. In one amazing play, Eli became a Super Bowl legend. Eli calmly broke free from the clutches of two defenders and fired the ball to wide receiver David Tyree. Leaping high above defenders, Tyree pinned the ball against his helmet for the catch. Eli had turned disaster into a game-changing first down. Four plays later, a touchdown pass to Plaxico Burress clinched the championship.

Eli manufactured another last-minute, game-winning drive in Super Bowl XLVI. He was named MVP in both Super Bowls. That's one more Super Bowl MVP than his big brother Peyton, if anyone is counting.

▶ **Joe Montana** is the quarterback that all others are measured against. Montana earned the nickname Joe Cool for his ability to snatch victory from likely defeat. Montana led his teams to an incredible 31 fourth quarter come-from-behind wins.

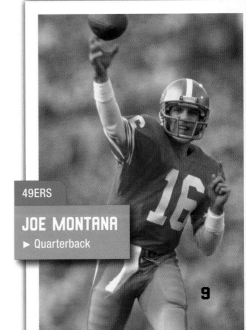

49ERS

JOE MONTANA
▶ Quarterback

HEIGHT: 6-2   WEIGHT: 200 lbs.
BORN: 6/11/1956, New Eagle, Pa.
SCOUTING REPORT: Ultimate big game quarterback seems at his calmest in the clutch.

49ERS

JERRY RICE
► Wide Receiver

HEIGHT: 6-2   WEIGHT: 200 lbs.
BORN: 10/13/1962, Crawford, Miss.
SCOUTING REPORT: Speedy master of route running is equally dangerous on slant patterns or sprinting deep for the long ball.

Montana pulled off one of his most memorable comebacks in Super Bowl XXIII after the 1988 season. Down 16–13 to the Cincinnati Bengals, the man in the Number 16 jersey led the San Francisco 49ers on an incredible 92-yard touchdown drive. With just 34 seconds on the clock, he hit John Taylor on a sharp 10-yard slant for the game-winning touchdown. Montana won four Super Bowls with the 49ers and earned three Super Bowl MVPs.

► **Jerry Rice** was the ultimate perfectionist. The speedy receiver's pass routes were models of precision. His cuts were razor-sharp. He could haul in an off-target pass without breaking stride. He could change speeds in an instant, leaving defenders grasping air.

Jerry earned an MVP trophy for his amazing Super Bowl XXIII performance. He ripped apart the Cincinnati Bengals defense for 11 receptions and 215 yards. Rice tormented NFL defenses for twenty seasons. When he was finished, he had rewritten the NFL record books. No NFL player has more career receiving yards, receptions, touchdowns, and all-purpose yards than Jerry Rice. No one is even close.

Today, ► **Terry Bradshaw** is known as the goofy NFL analyst on television every Sunday. But between 1970 and 1983, he was known as "the Blond Bomber."

Terry had a rocket for a right arm and a love for the deep ball. Bradshaw and his two outstanding receivers, Lynn Swann and John Stallworth, terrorized defensive backs. The trio was a threat to score from anywhere on the field.

With Bradshaw as quarterback, the Pittsburgh Steelers became one of the greatest teams in NFL history. They won four Super Bowls with Bradshaw garnering Super Bowl MVP honors in two of those championship games.

▶ **Bart Starr** commanded Vince Lombardi's army of Green Bay Packers. Starr led the Packers to victory in the first Super Bowl ever held on January 15, 1967. In all, he won five NFL titles.

In the 1967 NFC Championship game, a game called "The Ice Bowl" because the weather was a minus 13 degrees, Starr made one of football's boldest play calls. The Packers trailed the Dallas Cowboys 17–14 but were one yard from the goal line. Just 16 seconds remained. The Packers had no timeouts. A failed run would end the game, so the Cowboys were convinced Starr would pass the ball. Instead Starr kept the ball and dove in for the touchdown. It was a true quarterback sneak. Lombardi summed up the play perfectly, saying, "We gambled, and we won."

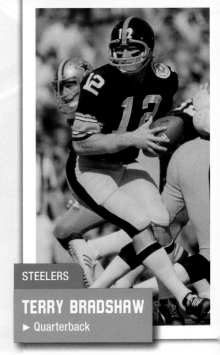

STEELERS

TERRY BRADSHAW
▶ Quarterback

HEIGHT: 6-3　　WEIGHT: 215 lbs.
BORN: 9/2/1948, Shreveport, La.
SCOUTING REPORT: Heady QB controls the action with smart play-calling and long bombs.

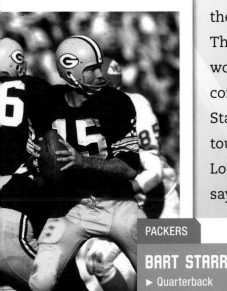

PACKERS

BART STARR
▶ Quarterback

HEIGHT: 6-1　　WEIGHT: 197 lbs.
BORN: 1/9/1934, Montgomery, Ala.
SCOUTING REPORT: Tough as nails quarterback always finds a way to win.

CHAPTER TWO

BARRY SANDERS
Was voted NFL MVP in 1997, as was Tomlinson in 2006.

LaDAINIAN TOMLINSON
Played majority of career with Chargers in California, same state where Lynch grew up.

EMMITT SMITH
All-time NFL rushing leader rivaled Sanders as the best running back of 1990s.

SIX DEGREES
OF MARSHAWN LYNCH

WALTER PAYTON
Rushed for NFL-record 26,726 yards—until Smith broke the record in 2002.

JAMES BROWN
Rushed for NFL-record 12,312 yards—until Payton broke the record in 1984.

GAME-BREAKING RUNNING BACKS

NFL defenses contain 11 of the fastest, strongest, and largest athletes in the world. When a running back takes a handoff, he becomes the target of all 11. Game-breaking NFL running backs love this attention. With amazing speed, agility, and power, they routinely perform amazing feats to stay on their feet.

▶ **Marshawn Lynch** started an earthquake in Seattle on January 8, 2011. Lynch took a handoff to the left. He ran over a couple New Orleans Saints defenders and broke into the open. Thirty-five yards downfield, Lynch threw another Saint defender to the ground. When he finally finished off his 67-yard touchdown run, Marshawn had broken nine tackles. Seahawks fans exploded. The roars from the stadium were so thunderous, they were recorded by a nearby seismometer. The run has become known as The Beast Quake. It's just one example of the incredible power on display when Marshawn enters Beast Mode.

SEAHAWKS

MARSHAWN LYNCH
▶ Running Back

HEIGHT: 5-11   WEIGHT: 215 lbs.
BORN: 4/22/1986, Oakland, Calif.
SCOUTING REPORT: Beast with the football in his arms never goes down easy.

▶ **LaDainian Tomlinson** was a touchdown machine for 11 years in the NFL. He found the end zone 10 times as a rookie and kept scoring touchdown after touchdown until he retired from the NFL in 2011.

CHARGERS

LaDAINIAN TOMLINSON
▶ Running Back

HEIGHT: 5-10   WEIGHT: 221 lbs.
BORN: 6/23/1979, Rosebud, Tex.
SCOUTING REPORT: Yard-gaining machine threatens defenses with diverse skills.

In 2006 Tomlinson led the San Diego Chargers to a 14–2 record, best in the league, and charged his way into NFL history. With 28 rushing touchdowns and three receiving touchdowns, L.T. crossed the goal line 31 times, an NFL single-season touchdown record.

Tomlinson was a triple threat. In addition to gaining yards by rushing, he was a dangerous receiver and a surprisingly good passer. In 2003 he was the first NFL player to rush for 1,000 yards and catch 100 passes. Tomlinson also tossed seven touchdown passes—quite an accomplishment for a running back—during his storied career.

▶ **Barry Sanders** was the most exciting running back in NFL history. Sanders didn't look very dangerous. At 5-feet-8 inches, under his shoulder pads, he looked like a pee-wee player. But during his 10 years with the Detroit Lions, Sanders was a nightmare for every defense in the NFL.

Sanders was a cut-back magician. He turned five-yard losses into touchdowns almost every week. He could pop out of the back of a pile of defenders as fast as he popped in. There was a method to his magic. "(I was able) to read the body language of a defender," Sanders said. "I almost had him on a string."

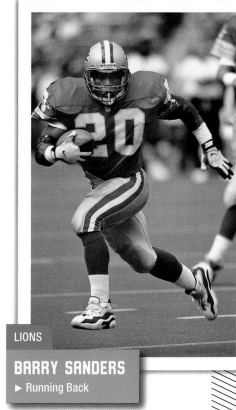

LIONS

BARRY SANDERS
▶ Running Back

HEIGHT: 5-8   WEIGHT: 203 lbs.
BORN: 7/16/1968, Wichita, Kan.
SCOUTING REPORT: Most elusive runner the NFL has ever seen has moves like some superhero waterbug.

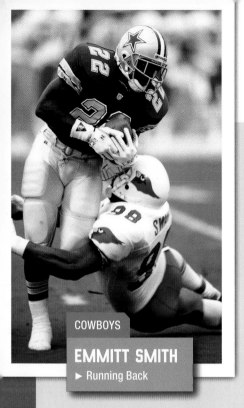

COWBOYS

EMMITT SMITH
▶ Running Back

HEIGHT: 5-9   WEIGHT: 221 lbs.
BORN: 5/15/1969, Pensacola, Fla.
SCOUTING REPORT: The perfect
all-purpose, non-stop running back.

▶ **Emmitt Smith** ran for more career yards than any NFL running back because he never quit.

His determination shined brightest during the last game of the 1993 season. Midway through the first quarter, Smith separated his shoulder. It was a serious injury, but he refused to stand on the sidelines. Darryl Johnston, the Dallas Cowboys fullback was amazed by his teammate's performance. "The stats he put up after that injury are unbelievable," Johnston said. Smith ran through the New York Giants for 170 yards. He also caught 10 passes for 62 yards. And he did most of it with one arm.

"Give me the heart of ▶ **Walter Payton**," said Jim Brown, NFL Hall of Fame running back. "There's never been a greater heart." Walter Payton's motto was "Never Die Easy." He did everything possible to keep a run alive.

BEARS

WALTER PAYTON
▶ Running Back

HEIGHT: 5-10 WEIGHT: 200 lbs.
BORN: 7/25/1953, Columbia, Miss.
SCOUTING REPORT: One-of-a-kind combo of
power and grace never runs out of bounds
before inflicting punishment on the D.

As running back for the Chicago Bears, Payton was the master of the stutter-step. He had a powerful stiff-arm. His acrobatic leaps into the end zone became legendary. When all else failed, Payton dropped his shoulder and drove through tacklers for extra yards. There was style and grace in everything Walter Payton did on the football field. He was the perfect definition of his nickname, Sweetness.

▶ **Jim Brown** was a freight train who played for the Cleveland Browns. The longer he ran, the faster he went. A long list of defenders regret ever stepping in front of that train.

Brown was only 29 years old when he retired. In just nine years, he won four league MVP trophies. He's the only player ever to average more than 100 yards per game.

Many still consider Brown to be the greatest running back to ever play. However, Brown never saw it that way. He said, "When running backs get into a room together, they don't argue about who is the best."

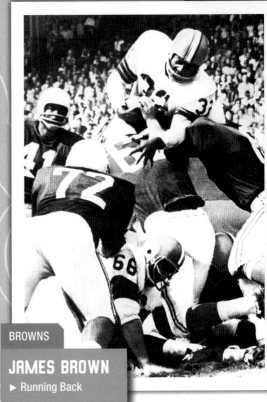

BROWNS

JAMES BROWN
▶ Running Back

HEIGHT: 6-2   WEIGHT: 232 lbs.
BORN: 2/17/1936, St. Simons Island, Ga.
SCOUTING REPORT: Unstoppable force of speed and power dominates defenses.

CHAPTER THREE

BRETT FAVRE
Won NFL MVP in 1995, 1996, and 1997, as Brady did in 2007 and 2010.

TOM BRADY
Sports jersey number 12, as does Luck.

DAN MARINO
Held NFL all-time records for completions, yards, and TDs until broken by Favre.

SIX DEGREES
OF ANDREW LUCK

FRAN TARKENTON
Held NFL all-time records for completions, yards, and TDs until broken by Marino.

JOE NAMATH
Played pro football in New York City like Tarkenton.

GUNSLINGERS

A great NFL quarterback is the rarest athlete in all of sports. Few athletes have the quick mind—not to mention the arm—required to fire a pass through a maze of defenders. Few sustain the courage needed to stand defenseless before a ferocious pass rush. And even fewer possess the leadership that inspires the faith of their teammates.

No rookie quarterback has entered the NFL with as many expectations as ▶ **Andrew Luck**. Entering the 2012 draft, experts compared Luck to NFL great John Elway. The Indianapolis Colts selected him with the first pick in the draft. Prior to making the pick, and knowing Luck was in store, the Colts had released longtime quarterback, Peyton Manning. Essentially, they chose the young Luck over an aging future Hall of Famer.

In week five of his rookie season, Luck proved that the Colts made the right decision. He guided the Colts to a comeback victory over the mighty Green Bay Packers. It was one of seven comeback wins for the 2012 Colts, after a 2–14 record the previous season. Luck led the Colts to the playoffs in 2012 and 2013. It seems the Colts may have found another Hall of Fame quarterback.

▶ **Tom Brady's** status among the NFL's all-time greatest quarterbacks isn't in doubt.

COLTS

ANDREW LUCK
▶ Quarterback

HEIGHT: 6-3   **WEIGHT:** 235 lbs.
BORN: 9/12/1989, Washington D.C.
SCOUTING REPORT: Size, speed, smarts, and a great arm make him instantly elite.

PATRIOTS

TOM BRADY
▶ Quarterback

HEIGHT: 6-4   **WEIGHT:** 225 lbs.
BORN: 8/3/1977, San Mateo, Calif.
TEAM: New England Patriots
SCOUTING REPORT: Master field general with a proven record is never unprepared.

However, in 2000, no one but Brady himself saw his fullest potential. Most scouts reported that Brady was slow on reads. He was slow to react. He didn't deliver the ball on time.

It didn't take long for Brady to get up to speed. In 2001, Brady led the New England Patriots to a championship. Since he became starting quarterback, the Patriots have missed the playoffs only twice. And they have won more games than any other NFL team. It would be hard to find anyone who thinks Tom Brady is slow anymore.

Few NFL players enjoyed playing football more than ▶ **Brett Favre**. He told jokes to the referees. He threw passes backhanded, underhanded, and sideways. After his teammates scored a touchdown, he ran into the end zone and tackled them. Favre also had a cannon on his right shoulder and a habit of making big plays.

Early in his career, Favre made a lot of incredible plays, but he also made a lot of mistakes. Soon he learned to control his reckless style. Favre earned three straight NFL MVP awards as a Green Bay Packer. "He drove you crazy," explained former Packers assistant coach, Steve Mariucci. "He made great plays. The place went wild."

PACKERS

BRETT FAVRE
▶ Quarterback

HEIGHT: 6-2   WEIGHT: 225 lbs.
BORN: 10/10/1969, Gulfport, Mo.
SCOUTING REPORT: Wild man on the field with a cannon for an arm plays the kind of fearless football fans love.

DAN MARINO
▶ Quarterback

HEIGHT: 6-4   WEIGHT: 224 lbs.
BORN: 9/15/1961, Pittsburgh, Pa.
SCOUTING REPORT: Strong arm and quick release means this quarterback can light up the scoreboard in a flash.

▶ **Dan Marino** and the Miami Dolphins' passing attack stunned the NFL. The Dolphins struck defenses fast, and they struck often. Marino had a lightning quick release for short passes. He had a strong arm for deep balls. When Marino was on the field, no part of the defense was safe.

Marino shredded the record books in 1984, his second NFL season. He threw 48 touchdown passes, 12 more than the previous record. And he became the first player to throw for more than 5,000 yards in one season. Marino's titanic records stood firm for more than 20 years.

If ▶ **Fran Tarkenton's** first receiver was covered, he looked for his second receiver. If his second receiver wasn't open, he looked to his third. If his third receiver was tied up, Tarkenton scrambled. He dodged tacklers and ran around behind the line of scrimmage until one of his

FRAN TARKENTON
▶ Quarterback

HEIGHT: 6-0   WEIGHT: 190 lbs.
BORN: 5/31/1943, Richmond, Va.
SCOUTING REPORT: Great scrambler keeps pla[y] alive until he finds the open receiver.

receivers broke open. Tarkenton scrambled so often, he became known as "The Mad Scrambler."

It's a great strategy if you can pull it off. And Tarkenton had all the tools. He could outrun most defenders. He also had an arsenal of fakes and spins to throw them off course. His strategy was extremely successful. Tarkenton led the Minnesota Vikings to three Super Bowls.

▶ **Joe Namath** had an explosive right arm and a personality to match. During his time with the New York Jets, Namath became the NFL's first celebrity. He was a tough, gritty quarterback on the field and a good-looking charmer off the field. He regularly popped up in magazine photos with beautiful Hollywood actresses on his arm. When he was injured, Namath paraded the sidelines in a fancy white fur coat. It wasn't long before the New York QB had earned the nickname "Broadway Joe."

Namath is famous for his bold guarantee of a Jets victory in Super Bowl III. Because he delivered that victory over the heavily favored Baltimore Colts, New York will always love Broadway Joe.

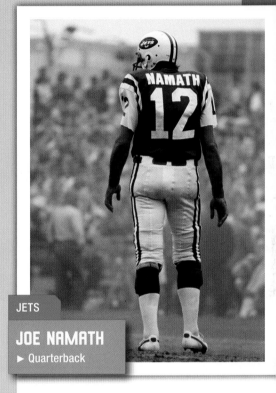

JETS

JOE NAMATH
▶ Quarterback

HEIGHT: 6-2   WEIGHT: 200 lbs.
BORN: 5/31/1943, Beaver Falls, Pa.
SCOUTING REPORT: Gritty quarterback shines brightest in the heat of the spotlight.

CHAPTER FOUR

TONY GONZALEZ
Played college basketball,
as did McNabb.

DONOVAN McNABB
Received votes in 1998 as a
nominee for the Heisman Trophy,
which Griffin won in 2011.

DEION SANDERS
Played pro baseball in
Atlanta, same city where
Gonzalez played pro football.

SIX DEGREES
OF ROBERT GRIFFIN III

BO JACKSON
Star college football player
played both pro football and
baseball, as did Sanders.

JIM THORPE
Star footballer also spent time playing
pro baseball as a star outfielder,
as did Jackson.

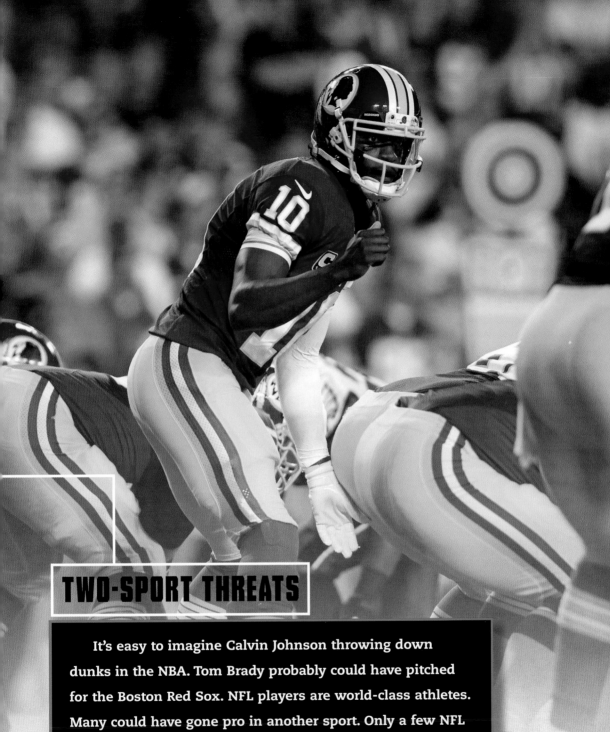

TWO-SPORT THREATS

It's easy to imagine Calvin Johnson throwing down dunks in the NBA. Tom Brady probably could have pitched for the Boston Red Sox. NFL players are world-class athletes. Many could have gone pro in another sport. Only a few NFL players possessed the talent and determination to become actual multi-sport threats.

Robert Griffin III is a deluxe model of the new, advanced NFL quarterback. Griffin, fondly known as RG3, has all the traditional tools of a drop back quarterback. He has a strong arm and a quick mind. But unlike traditional quarterbacks, RG3 is usually the best all-around athlete on the field.

Athletic quarterbacks like RG3, Colin Kaepernick, and Cam Newton have revolutionized the position. They are extremely dangerous through the air and on the ground. They force opposing teams to defend every part of the field.

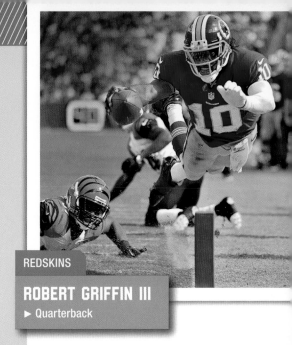

REDSKINS

ROBERT GRIFFIN III
▶ Quarterback

HEIGHT: 6-2   WEIGHT: 220 lbs.
BORN: 2/12/1990, Okinawa, Japan
SCOUTING REPORT: Tremendous athlete has scary quarterback skills to burn.

RG3's tremendous athletic ability was on full display at Baylor University. He won the Heisman Trophy as quarterback of the football team. RG3 was also a track star. He was one race away from the Olympics in the 400-meter hurdles.

Donovan McNabb brought incredible athleticism—and the frame of a linebacker— to the quarterback position when he came into

EAGLES

DONOVAN McNABB
▶ Quarterback

HEIGHT: 6-2   WEIGHT: 240 lbs.
BORN: 11/25/1976, Chicago, Ill.
SCOUTING REPORT: Outstanding field general brings great size and bruising capabilities to the QB position.

the NFL as a member of the Philadelphia Eagles in 1999. He gave Philly fans reason to cheer as soon as he donned a winged helmet of green. His sharp passes, rugged rambles, and great leadership made the Eagles an early-2000s NFL powerhouse.

Immediate success in the NFL was just a continuation of excellence for McNabb. In college, he played for the 1996 national championship—in basketball! As a reserve guard, McNabb was a valuable contributer for the Syracuse University Orangemen for two years before giving up hoops to focus on the gridiron.

Growing up in Huntington Beach, California, ▸ **Tony Gonzalez** never dreamed of NFL glory. Young Tony's first love was basketball. A bruiser under the basket, he pulled down rebound after rebound.

Gonzalez played both basketball and football at the University of California, Berkeley. He loved basketball, but his star shined brightest as a tight end. Gonzalez played 16 seasons in the NFL and became one the league's all-time greatest tight ends. His basketball skills did come in handy on the football field. Like a great rebounder, he could keep defenders on his back in order to get open and catch a pass. Thus, no matter how tight the coverage, Tony Gonzalez could always haul in the catch. After catching touchdowns, Gonzalez's signature end zone celebration was the over-the-goalpost slam dunk.

FALCONS
TONY GONZALEZ
▸ Tight End

HEIGHT: 6-5   WEIGHT: 251 lbs.
BORN: 2/27/1976, Torrance, Calif.
SCOUTING REPORT: Big tight end with soft hands is always in the right spot.

No professional football player loved dancing like ▶ **Deion Sanders**. It was Sanders' custom to follow most of his accomplishments with a dance. He danced after touchdowns, interceptions, receptions, and incompletions. Sometimes he danced after a dance.

When he wasn't dancing, "Prime Time" was employed as the NFL's best shutdown cornerback. He also found time to be an explosive kick returner and a receiver.

Sanders was also a fine Major Leaguer. In 1989, he hit a home run and scored a touchdown in the same week. Sanders is the only person to play in the World Series and the Super Bowl.

▶ **Bo Jackson** was a modern-day Paul Bunyan. But unlike Paul Bunyan's tall tales, Bo's unbelievable feats are recorded on video. It's a good thing. If you didn't see Bo in action, you wouldn't believe the stories.

We can watch Bo snap a bat over his head like a toothpick. We can watch him flatten NFL linebackers like a 4x4 truck running over a soda can.

Bo is the first and only person to become a Pro Bowler in the National Football League and an All-Star in the Major Leagues.

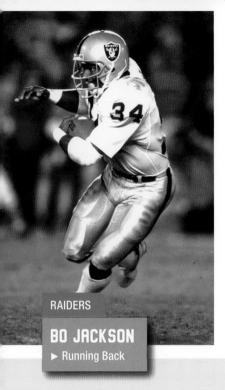

RAIDERS

BO JACKSON
▶ Running Back

HEIGHT: 6-1   WEIGHT: 227 lbs.
BORN: 11/30/1962, Bessemer, Ala.
SCOUTING REPORT: One of the greatest athletes of all time—in any sport—simply dazzles with insane raw power, speed, and instinct.

His career was cut short by a terrible hip injury suffered on the gridiron. Luckily, Bo gave us plenty of tall tales to watch.

▶ **Jim Thorpe** amazed King Gustav V of Sweden in the 1912 Olympics. Thorpe easily won gold in the decathlon and the pentathlon. At the medal ceremony, the king told Jim, "You, sir, are the greatest athlete in the world." Jim simply said, "Thanks, King."

No one would disagree with King Gustav. Thorpe's phenomenal accomplishments remain unmatched. In addition to his two gold medals, Thorpe played lacrosse, barnstormed with a professional basketball team, and played six years as an outfielder in the Major Leagues. But football was Thorpe's first love, and football fans loved him. For more than 20 years, fans packed football stadiums just to watch him play.

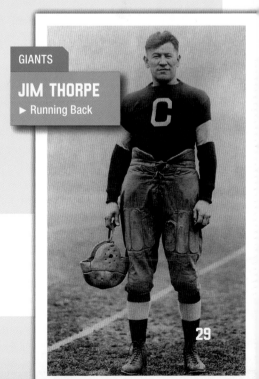

GIANTS

JIM THORPE
▶ Running Back

HEIGHT: 6-1   WEIGHT: 202 lbs.
BORN: 5/22/1887, Prague, Okla.
SCOUTING REPORT: "Greatest athlete in the world" plays many sports, but heart belongs to football.

CHAPTER FIVE

J.J. WATT
As a collegian, won the
2011 Lott Trophy, an award
named for Ronnie Lott.

RONNIE LOTT
Led NFL in interceptions in 1986
and 1991, like Richard Sherman
did in 2013.

REGGIE WHITE
Single season sack leader in
1987 and 1988, like Taylor
(1986) and Watt (2012).

SIX DEGREES
OF RICHARD SHERMAN

LAWRENCE TAYLOR
Competed at Wrestlemania XI,
with White sitting ringside
for support.

DEACON JONES
After playing days, enjoyed
part-time work as an actor,
as did Taylor.

DEVASTATING DEFENDERS

Offenses attack. Their goal is to push the football across their opponents' goal line. Defenses protect. Their goal is to protect their team's goal line. Strange as it sounds, the most devastating defenders protect their goal line by attacking. If offenses can't stop these attackers, they won't be able to attack. Offenses must avoid, double-team, or even triple-team these devastating defenders.

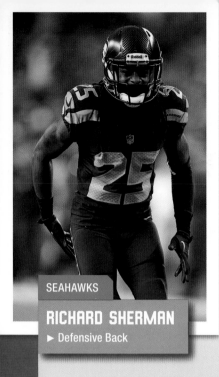

SEAHAWKS

RICHARD SHERMAN
▶ Defensive Back

HEIGHT: 6-3   WEIGHT: 195 lbs.
BORN: 3/30/1988, Compton, Calif.
SCOUTING REPORT: Fast-talking, hard-working, shutdown cornerback is afraid of no one.

▶ **Richard Sherman** of the Seattle Seahawks was raised by hard-working parents. He graduated from Stanford, California's most prestigious university. With his upbringing, it's not surprising that he became one of the NFL's top cornerbacks. However, it is surprising that he became the NFL's undisputed king of trash talk.

Sherman loves to talk. He is a hyper-energetic, competitive chatterbox. His high school coach, Keith Donerson, discovered this quickly. "Sometimes I'd … tell Richard to stop talking in practice," recalled Donerson. "And he'd go into the tank."

No one is safe from Sherman's tireless taunts. Receivers, quarterbacks, and coaches are all fair game. He gets into their heads and throws them off their games. And more often than not, Sherman comes out on top.

▶ **Ronnie Lott** believed that he could change a football game with one ferocious hit. In Super Bowl XXIII, the

49ERS

RONNIE LOTT
▶ Safety

HEIGHT: 6-0   WEIGHT: 203 lbs.
BORN: 5/8/1959, Albuquerque, N.M.
SCOUTING REPORT: Punishing defensive back has a nose for interceptions.

hard-hitting defensive back proved his theory to be true.

The San Francisco 49ers were up against the Cincinnati Bengals' high-powered offense. In the first quarter, the Bengals were pushing the 49ers down the field. Then Lott came up on a run play and crushed Bengals running back Icky Woods. The 49ers team bench exploded with celebration like they'd won the game on that play alone. Lott and his 49er teammates rode the momentum from the big hit to a Super Bowl championship.

▶ **J.J. Watt** always had the athletic ability and size to be a good defensive lineman. He became one of the best because he never stopped working hard. Watt's coach at the University of Wisconsin, Bret Bielema, learned the secret to Watt's success. Bielema explained, "He's at his strongest when other people are at their weakest." By that, Bielema meant that J.J. Watt never quits on a play, even when it's late in the game or a play is seemingly over.

If he doesn't get to the quarterback, Watt doesn't stop. He batted down an incredible 16 passes for the Houston Texans during the 2012 season. No defensive lineman had ever batted down more than 11 passes in a season. Now he goes by the name J.J. Swatt.

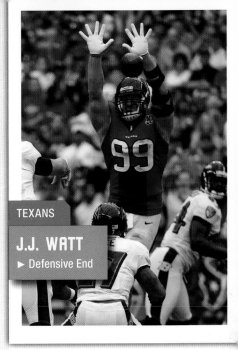

TEXANS

J.J. WATT
▶ Defensive End

HEIGHT: 6-6 WEIGHT: 290 lbs.
BORN: 3/22/1989, Pewaukee, Wisc.
SCOUTING REPORT: Monstrous, game-changing defensive lineman is a sack and pass-tipping machine.

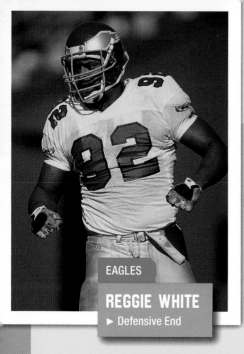

EAGLES

REGGIE WHITE
► Defensive End

HEIGHT: 6-5   WEIGHT: 300 lbs.
BORN: 12/19/1961, Chattanooga, Tenn.
SCOUTING REPORT: Unstoppable, fast-moving
mountain anchors any defensive line.

► **Reggie White** was ordained as a minister at the age of 17. During his NFL career, he was known as "The Minister of Defense." But he showed opposing offenses absolutely no mercy. With the Philadelphia Eagles, White recorded 124 sacks in 121 games.

White was a behemoth. He stood 6-foot-5 and weighed 300 pounds. Despite his enormous size, White was as quick as a cat. No one offensive lineman in the NFL could block him. "We had to double Reggie White every single snap," said coach Mike Holmgren, who coached White for six seasons in Green Bay after White left Philadelphia. "Otherwise, he could single-handedly take over the game."

There's an old clip of ► **Lawrence Taylor** stalking the sidelines. His eyes are glowing like dark rocks of fire. He yells to his teammates, "Let's go out there like a bunch of crazed dogs." Then he adds, "And have some fun."

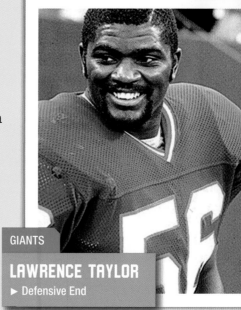

GIANTS

LAWRENCE TAYLOR
► Defensive End

HEIGHT: 6-3   WEIGHT: 237 lbs.
BORN: 2/4/1959, Williamsburg, Va.
SCOUTING REPORT: Full-throttle linebacker uses incredible speed for sledgehammer hits.

Lawrence Taylor—or LT, as he was simply known—played like a crazed dog. He was hungry for quarterbacks and running backs. LT threw his entire body into every play. As a linebacker for the New York Giants, he tore apart NFL offenses for 13 years. He tossed aside 300-pound lineman like ragdolls. Then he exploded into ball carriers and wiped them out. A crazed dog never had so much fun.

▶ **Deacon Jones** loved tackling quarterbacks behind the line of scrimmage. He loved it so much, he coined the phrase by which the play has been known ever since. Deacon named his favorite activity the "sack."

In his prime with the Los Angeles Rams, Jones was remarkably good at sacking the quarterback. His signature move—the head slap—involved Jones slapping offensive lineman upside their helmet. While they were off-balance, he ran by them and sacked the quarterback. The head slap was so unstoppable, the NFL finally made it illegal.

Unfortunately, the NFL didn't start recording sacks until 1982. Jones retired in 1974. Though Jones' sack total can only be estimated, his contribution to the game football is unmistakable.

CHARGERS

DEACON JONES
▶ Defensive End

HEIGHT: 6-5   WEIGHT: 271 lbs.
BORN: 12/9/1938, Eatonville, Fla.
SCOUTING REPORT: One of the first big, agile defensive lineman is the original king of sacks.

CHAPTER SIX

LARRY FITZGERALD
At 6-foot-3 and 225 pounds, a mirror image of Thomas' physical dimensions.

DEMARYIUS THOMAS
Played college football at Georgia Tech, as did Johnson.

RANDY MOSS
Played first seven seasons for Vikings, for whom Fitzgerald was a ball boy.

SIX DEGREES
OF CALVIN JOHNSON

LYNN SWANN
Consensus All-American in college at USC in 1973, like Moss was at Marshall in 1997.

DON HUTSON
Played on a Collegiate National Championship team (Alabama 1934) like Swann (USC 1972).

TOP FLIGHT RECEIVERS

Air attacks continue to become more and more important in the NFL. Throwing the ball forces defenses to defend short, deep, and from sideline to sideline. Most wide receivers specialize in attacking certain parts of the field. Some are possession receivers. Some are deep threats. Top flight receivers are full-field threats.

CALVIN JOHNSON
▶ Wide Receiver

HEIGHT: **6-5** WEIGHT: **239 lbs.**
BORN: **9/25/1985, Tyrone, Ga.**
SCOUTING REPORT: **The perfect receiver: fast, tall, great hands, can outjump any cornerback.**

Let's pretend there's a laboratory deep beneath the Pro Football Hall of Fame in Canton, Ohio. Inside, the world's greatest scientists are constructing the perfect wide receiver. They carefully follow a blueprint drawn up by Roger Staubach and Johnny Unitas. After years of tireless work, the scientists emerge with their creation. In this story, their creation could only be a clone of ▶ **Calvin Johnson**.

At 6-feet-5-inches, Johnson, also known as Megatron, towers over defensive backs. His arms are extremely long, and his hands are nearly the size of tennis rackets. Unlike other big receivers, he is sports-car fast and can leap out of the stadium. Johnson can outrun or outjump every defensive back in the NFL. Johnson's sort of perfection seems nearly unfair.

▶ **Demaryius Thomas** is a man-child. The beefy receiver can push through defenders. He can adjust to the ball in the air. And he's fast enough to take a simple screen pass to the house. Thomas's career exploded in 2012—his third season with the Broncos—when legendary quarterback Peyton Manning joined the team. Manning and Thomas quickly became one of the league's deadliest combinations. In 2013 Thomas caught 14 of Manning's single-season NFL record 55 touchdown passes and helped Denver reach the Super Bowl.

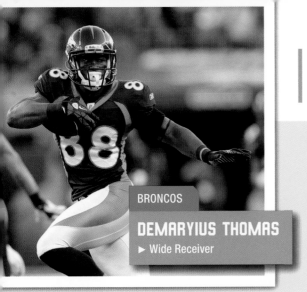

BRONCOS
DEMARYIUS THOMAS
▶ Wide Receiver

HEIGHT: 6-3　　WEIGHT: 229 lbs.
BORN: 12/25/1987, Montrose, Ga.
SCOUTING REPORT: Powerful young receiver
with breakaway speed is on the road to stardom.

If defenses don't give Thomas extra attention, the Broncos might just break the scoreboard. Even when Thomas is surrounded by defenders, he is dangerous. Of course it doesn't hurt that one of the best passers in the game has confidence in him.

If the ball is thrown anywhere in ▶ **Larry Fitzgerald's** zip code, it's his. Fitzgerald's hands are like vise grips. Quite routinely, he snags passes out of the air with just one hand. And he does it while defenders claw and scratch at the ball.

"Defensive backs are taught to rake and smack and grab and pull and tug your hands away from the football at all times," said Fitzgerald. "You have to have really strong hands to get the ball, and then you have to tuck it away really quickly."

Making highlight reel catches is just part of Larry Fitzgerald's everyday life.

HEIGHT: 6-3　　WEIGHT: 225 lbs.
BORN: 8/31/1983, Minneapolis, Minn.
SCOUTING REPORT: Technically gifted
receiver with the best hands in the game.

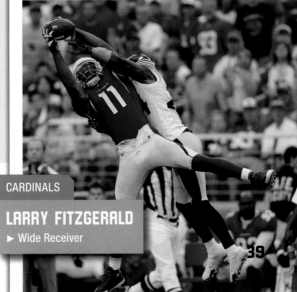

CARDINALS
LARRY FITZGERALD
▶ Wide Receiver

HEIGHT: 6-4   WEIGHT: 215 lbs.
BORN: 2/13/1977, Rand, W.Va.
SCOUTING REPORT: Incredibly dangerous receiver threatens to score from anywhere on the field.

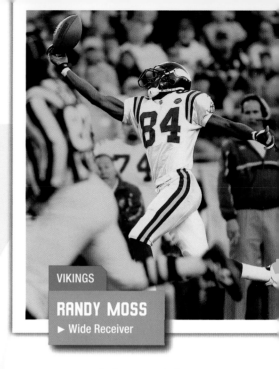

VIKINGS
RANDY MOSS
▶ Wide Receiver

▶ **Randy Moss** was the centerpiece of two of the greatest offenses in NFL history. In 1998 Moss led a record-breaking Minnesota Vikings offense in touchdowns and receiving yards. In 2007 Moss played with Tom Brady and the New England Patriots. The Patriots broke the 1998 Vikings' record for most points in a season. Moss set the single-season record for receiving touchdowns with 23.

Moss might be the single most dangerous weapon in the history of football. With his otherworldly speed, Moss could score from any place on the field at any moment in the game. A Hail Mary in Moss' direction was considered a safe play.

Football is considered a ferocious activity played by daring athletes. Dance is considered an elegant craft for those with artistic natures. The two rarely cross paths. ▶ **Lynn Swann** proved that dancing and football can be a pretty pair. Lynn took dance

STEELERS
LYNN SWANN
▶ Wide Receiver

HEIGHT: 5-11 WEIGHT: 180 lbs.
BORN: 3/7/1952, Alcoa, Tenn.
SCOUTING REPORT: Seems to dance in the air when he goes airborne for a catch.

lessons throughout his childhood. As an adult he became a Hall of Fame wide receiver. He credited dance lessons with helping him master the art of body control, balance, rhythm, and timing.

No one played football with more grace. Swann ran like a stallion and jumped like a deer. While defenders fell to Earth, he remained floating in the air.

▶ **Don Hutson**, the Alabama Antelope, played for the Green Bay Packers from 1935 until 1945. In those days, teams believed pass plays were risky. Defenses were allowed to rough up receivers. An interception was almost as likely as a completion.

Single-handedly, Hutson made the NFL believe in the forward pass. On Hutson's first NFL play, he caught an 83-yard touchdown pass. For the next 11 seasons, he wrote the manual on how to play wide receiver. He was the first receiver to run precise pass routes. When he retired, Hutson had more than doubled nearly every NFL receiving record.

PACKERS

DON HUTSON
▶ Wide Receiver

HEIGHT: 6-1   WEIGHT: 183 lbs.
BORN: 1/31/1913, Pine Bluff, Ark.
SCOUTING REPORT: Authors the book on how to play receiver in the NFL.

SIX DEGREES TRIVIA >>>>>

1. Which three quarterbacks were born in the state of Pennsylvania?
2. Which player has the most NFL MVP seasons?
3. Which two receivers attended Georgia Tech University?
4. Which players won the Heisman Trophy?
5. Which three players have held the NFL's career rushing yards record?
6. Which four players have won four Super Bowls?
7. Which two quarterbacks squared off in Super Bowl IX?
8. Which player was the first player to win two Super Bowl MVPs?
9. Which five players were the number one overall pick in their respective drafts?
10. Which four players were born in California?
11. Which two players were winning teammates in Super Bowl XXXI?
12. Which player was a member of the Los Angeles Rams' "Fearsome Foursome"?
13. Which five players played on an NCAA National Champion football team?
14. Which player was a descendant of the great Sauk and Fox chief Black Hawk?
15. Which quarterbacks faced off in two Super Bowls?

MATCH THE PLAYER WITH HIS NICKNAME

1.	JOE MONTANA	MEGATRON
2.	MARSHAWN LYNCH	THE MAD SCRAMBLER
3.	WALTER PAYTON	SUPER FREAK
4.	JOE NAMATH	PRIME TIME
5.	FRAN TARKENTON	LT
6.	ROBERT GRIFFIN	RG3
7.	DEION SANDERS	BEAST MODE
8.	LAWRENCE TAYLOR	BOADWAY JOE
9.	REGGIE WHITE	JOE COOL
10.	CALVIN JOHNSON	SWEETNESS
11.	RANDY MOSS	THE MINISTER OF DEFENSE

ANSWERS

Word Bank Answers:
1. Joe Montana, Dan Marino, and Joe Namath; 2. Peyton Manning (5); 3. Demaryius Thomas and Calvin Johnson; 4. Robert Griffin III (2011), Barry Sanders (1988), Bo Jackson (1985); 5. Jim Brown, Walter Payton, and Emmitt Smith; 6. Lynn Swann, Ronnie Lott, Terry Bradshaw, Jerry Rice, and Joe Montana; 7. Fran Tarkenton and Terry Bradshaw; 8. Bart Starr; 9. Andrew Luck, Eli Manning, Peyton Manning, Bo Jackson, and Terry Bradshaw; 10. Marshawn Lynch, Tom Brady, Tony Gonzalez, and Richard Sherman, 11. Brett Favre and Reggie White; 12. Deacon Jones; 13. Joe Namath (University of Alabama 1964), Joe Montana (University of Notre Dame, 1977), Don Hutson (University of Alabama, 1934), Lynn Swann (University of Southern California, 1972), Ronnie Lott (University of Southern California, 1978), 14. Jim Thorp; 15. Tom Brady and Eli Manning

Nickname Trivia Answers:
1. Joe Cool, 2. Beast Mode, 3. Sweetness, 4. Boadway Joe, 5. The Mad Scrambler, 6. RG3, 7. Prime Time, 8. LT, 9. The Minister of Defense, 10. Megatron, 11. Super Freak

43

BIG CONNECTIONS

Became a full-time starter in 2001

Quarterbacks born in Pennsylvania

University of Alabama

Actors

Jersey #10

Jersey #34

ANDREW LUCK
JOE NAMATH
FRAN TARKENTON
TOM BRADY
BRETT FAVRE
DAN MARINO

MARSHAWN LYNCH
JAMES BROWN
WALTER PAYTON
LADAINIAN TOMLINSON
BARRY SANDERS
EMMITT SMITH

PEYTON MANNING
BART STARR
TERRY BRADSHAW
ELI MANNING
JOE MONTANA
JERRY RICE

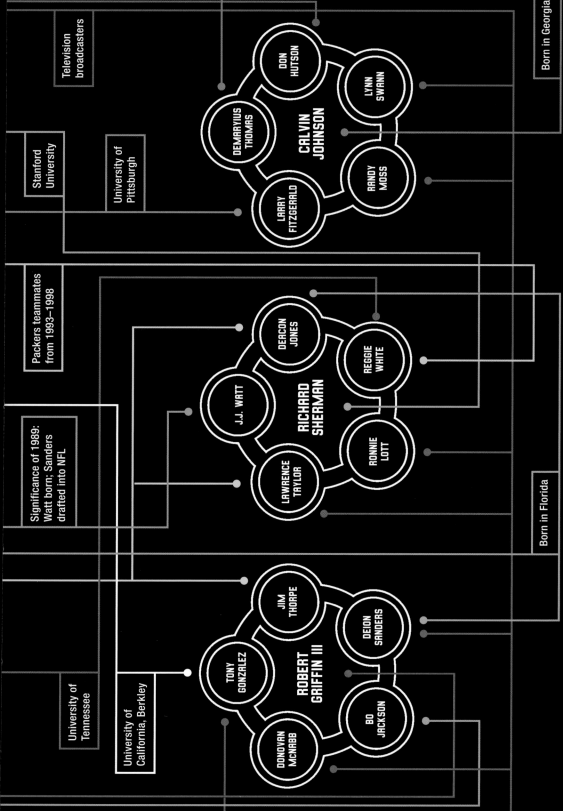

GLOSSARY

ACL and MCL—two ligaments, bands of tissue, that hold the bones in the knee together

all-purpose yards—rushing, receiving, and return yards combined

barnstorm—a traveling athletic team that plays exhibition games

drop back quarterback—a quarterback that mostly drops back into the pocket to throws a pass

Hail Mary—a long pass with a small chance of success usually thrown at the end of the game

line of scrimmage—an imaginary line, parallel to the goal line, where the offense starts a play; a player can not throw a pass after crossing the line of scrimmage with the ball

pass routes—the path run by a receiver during a play

pass rush—the movement of the defensive players toward the quarterback

pocket—the area behind the offensive line where the quarterback sets up to throw a pass

possession receivers—receivers that are good at running short routes and catching passes in heavy traffic

reads—the ability to determine if a receiver is covered

rehabilitation—to restore something to good condition

seismometer—a device that measures movements that occur in the Earth

shutdown cornerback—a cornerback that is so good that the receivers they cover almost never catch a pass

slant—a pass route in which the receiver runs straight upfield and cuts into the middle of the field on an angle

stiff-arm—extending and arm to hold off a tackler

stutter-step—a sudden change in speed intended to fool chasing defenders

trash-talk—boastful or unfavorable speech used to disturb opponents

vision—the ability to see where and when a hole will open at the line of scrimmage

READ MORE

Biskup, Agnieszka. *Football: How It Works.* The Science of Sports. North Mankato, Minn.: Capstone Press, 2010.

Doeden, Matt. *The World's Greatest Football Players.* North Mankato, Minn.: Capstone Press, 2010.

Frederick, Shane. *Football: The Math of the Game.* Sports Math. North Mankato, Minn.: Capstone Press, 2011.

INTERNET SITES

FactHound offers a safe, fun way to find Internet sites related to this book. All of the sites on FactHound have been researched by our staff.

Here's all you do:

Visit *www.facthound.com*

Type in this code: 9781491421451

 **Super-cool stuff!** Check out projects, games and lots more at **www.capstonekids.com**

INDEX